WHAT SHOES WILL YOU wear?

Activity & Idea Book

published by

NATIONAL CENTER for
YOUTH ISSUES

Where do I start?
There are seven steps to career exploration.

The activities in this book are designed to teach these seven steps and model the process that all must travel through when searching for the career that fits your "sole" the best!

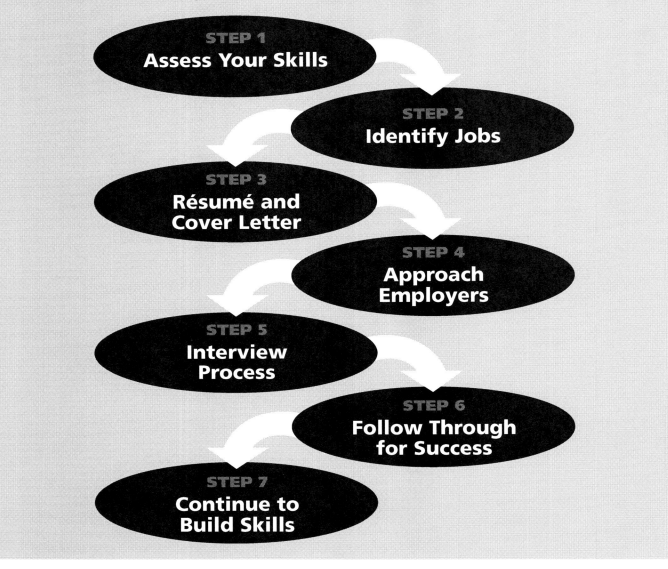

STEP 1
Assess Your Skills

STEP 2
Identify Jobs

STEP 3
Résumé and Cover Letter

STEP 4
Approach Employers

STEP 5
Interview Process

STEP 6
Follow Through for Success

STEP 7
Continue to Build Skills

Duplication and Copyright

Summary: A supplementary teacher's guide for *What Shoes Will You Wear.*
Full of discussion questions and exercises to share with students.

Written by: Julia Cook • Illustrations by: Anita DuFalla • Published by National Center for Youth Issues
Printed at Starkey Printing • Chattanooga, TN, USA • February 2018

NATIONAL CENTER for YOUTH ISSUES

P.O. Box 22185 • Chattanooga, TN 37422-2185
423.899.5714 • 866.318.6294 • fax: 423.899.4547 • www.ncyi.org
ISBN: 978-1-937870-35-5

Beginning of the Year Career Assessment

Name_____

Directions

Complete all the questions below.

1. The most important factor in selecting a career is:

☐ **a.** Pay

☐ **b.** Where I work (inside/outside)

☐ **c.** Who I work with

☐ **d.** If my skills match what is required

2. I know how to research/look up information about my career. ☐ Yes ☐ No

3. I know what is on a job application. ☐ Yes ☐ No

4. The word "wages" means _____.

5. Résumés include information about a job. ☐ True ☐ False

6. One thing to remember on a job interview is _____.

The Big List in Action!!!

Objective

- Identify concrete examples of people demonstrating possession of the skills and qualities on the Big List. (i.e. Team spirit – cheered on my teammates when I was not playing.)
- Increase awareness of the Big List in action!

1. My Qualities and Skills

Using The Big List Worksheet, give an example of how **YOU** have demonstrated each quality and skill.

2. The Qualities and Skills of Others

Using the second copy of The Big List Worksheet, ask other people (family and friends) for examples of how **THEY** have demonstrated each quality and skill. You may ask as many people as you would like when completing this activity but **make sure you list the name of the person next to their response**.

✂ cut along dotted lines

The BIG List Worksheet

Communication Skills _____

Listening Skills _____

Reading _____

Writing _____

Science _____

Social Studies _____

Math _____

Creative Thinking _____

Good Reasoning Skills _____

Decision Making Skills _____

Problem Solving Skills _____

Desire to Never Stop Learning _____

Be Responsible _____

Be On Time _____

Self-confidence _____

Integrity _____

Motivation _____

Flexibility _____

Team Spirit _____

Good Work Attitude _____

Be Honest _____

Cooperate With Others _____

Have Self Control _____

Good Social Skills _____

Well-groomed _____

My Self-Assessment

Objective

Students will identify some of their personal interests and skills which may help them when exploring different careers.

Materials

• My Self-Assessment Worksheet
• Pencil or pen

Directions

1. Working independently, answer the following questions to help identify some of the things you like to do, some things you are good at, and some things that interest you.

2. **Important:** There are no wrong answers!

My Self- Assessment Worksheet

Ten things that I enjoy doing:

_____

_____

Some things that come easy for me to do (my strengths) include:

_____

_____

Some things that are hard for me to do (my weaknesses) include:

_____

_____

Some things I find really exciting/interesting are:

To me, The most important factor in selecting a career is:

☐ **a.** Pay   ☐ **c.** Who I work with

☐ **b.** Where I work (inside/outside)   ☐ **d.** If my skills match what is required

Right now, my dream job would be:

_____

_____

Shoes in the Middle!

Objective

Students will learn about various professions and identify which shoes are worn in certain professions.

Directions

1. Divide students into two teams (A and B), and let each team come up with a team name.

2. Have each team place the shoes that they brought in a pile in front of the room.

3. Have one team member from Team A hold up a shoe from Team A's pile. Using the question list below, Team B can ask any five questions about the shoe owner's profession.

4. Team B then works together and comes up with a guess of what the owner of the shoe does for a living. If they are right, they get a point. If not, the shoe is placed back into Team A's pile.

5. Have one member of Team B hold up a shoe and repeat as stated above.

6. The first team to 5 points wins.

7. If the shoe is not guessed correctly and is returned to the pile, it can be used again by asking different questions. Remember to take good notes on the questions that have been previously asked!

Materials

- One shoe from home from mom, dad, or other family member
- Shoes in the Middle Question Sheet (below)
- Pen or pencil
- Paper for note taking

Shoes in the Middle Question Sheet

1. Does the person work mostly outside or inside?
2. Does the person sit at a desk a lot of the time?
3. Does the person work with his/her hands?
4. How much schooling did the person have to have to get this job?
5. Does the person have a college degree of any kind?
   If so, what kind of degree: Trade School Certification or Degree, Bachelor's Degree, Master's Degree, Doctorate, etc.?
6. Does the person sell things?
7. Does the person work with tools?
8. Does the person drive a company car or vehicle?
9. What is the typical work schedule for this person?
10. How long does it take this person to get to work?
11. Does this person have to travel a lot?
12. FREE QUESTION – Make up a question of your own.

A Means to an END

Objective

1. Students will be able to identify important skillsets needed that match up with their career interests.
2. Students will choose a skill that they are interested in improving upon and create a plan to achieve mastering that skill.

Materials
- Pencil
- Goal Worksheet

Directions

Fill out the worksheet below and discuss your responses as a group.

My Goal Worksheet
When setting a goal remember the basics!

- Set a goal that you can actually achieve.
- Plan steps to reach your goal.
- Be able to measure your goal. (How will you know you've accomplished it?)
- Practice your goal.

- Use positive Self-Talk. (Tell yourself that you can reach your goal!)
- Give your best effort when trying to reach your goal.
- Reflect on your progress. (Ask yourself, "Did I reach my goal?")

1. When I grow up, I want to be a _____ .

2. To become a _____, I must have the following three skills:
    - _____
    - _____
    - _____

3. My goal to help me achieve one of these skills is:_____
    _____

4. My goal is reasonable and reachable because I can: _____
    _____

5. My plan for reaching my goal is:_____
    _____

6. I can practice my plan by: _____
    _____

7. I am using positive self-talk when I:_____
    _____

8. I am putting forth my best effort in reaching my goal because I am:_____
    _____

9. I will know when I have met my goal when I can: _____
    _____

Persuasive Career Fair

Objective

Students research a career of choice and prepare a persuasive project for that career. Students will present their projects orally during a class career fair.

Directions

1. Pair up students with similar career interests.

2. Have each pair choose a career and design a project (e.g. poem, letter, artistic display, poster, power point presentation, etc.) that promotes their career of choice and persuades others to potentially consider choosing that career in the future.

3. Include information about the importance of the career to society, type of work that is included, training that is needed, location (indoor/outdoor) in which employees may work, number of hours per week that is required, stories of experts in the field, etc.

4. Have teams promote careers of choice by presenting their projects to the rest of the class (and perhaps other classes as well).

5. Have students vote on the top three persuasive presentations.

6. Discuss as a class what made different information in each project more or less interesting to you.

7. Display projects throughout the classroom and invite parents and other guests in to view and hear presentations.

Materials

- Audio/visual equipment
- Poster presentation board
- Art supplies as needed
- Guest speakers (optional)

My Career Reflection

Objective

Students will learn about and present many different factors that go into a particular job of interest and also one of disinterest.

Directions

Have students draw or print off a picture of what their FAVORITE and LEAST FAVORITE careers look like and present their information to the class.

Have students fill out the career information sheets (below) and display them along with the pictures for all to see on two separate bulletin boards: (1) *Careers We Like the Most and Why* (2) *Careers We Like the Least and Why*.

Choose the career that is MOST INTERESTING to you and fill out the following information:

Career: _____

a. In this career, I might expect to spend most of my time working where? _____

_____

b. For this career, I would need to _____ after finishing high school.

c. A subject in school that would be important for this job is _____.

d. One of the reasons I am most interested in this career is _____

_____.

Choose a career that is the LEAST INTERESTING to you and fill out the following information:

Career: _____

a. In this career, I would spend most of my time working where? _____

_____

b. For this career, I would need to do _____ after finishing high school.

c. A subject in school that would be important for this job is _____.

d. One of the reasons I am not interested in this career at all is it _____

_____.

My Symbolic Career Collage

Objective

Students will identify and research a career of interest and create a collage consisting of five different symbols that represent that career- including what "shoes" a person might wear.

Directions

1. Choose a career of interest without telling anyone what it is.

2. Research your career choice and find out interesting facts about it.

3. Search through your stuff at home, including old magazines and other picture sources, garage sales and thrift shops to find five symbols that represent your career. Make sure you include a picture of what kind of shoes are worn.

4. Cut and creatively paste these items onto the poster board.

5. Describe your collage in detail without telling what your career is by explaining each item and how it relates to your career choice.

6. Ask the group to guess what your career choice is.

7. Explain why you chose the career that you did.

8. Answer any questions the group might have about your career choice.

9. Display your collage for all to admire.

Materials
- Old magazines
- Photos
- Trinkets
- Clip art
- Scissors
- Poster board
- Glue sticks

Career Guess Who

Objective

- Students will be able to identify different careers by listening to clues that describe each career.
- Students will be exposed to new language associated with particular careers.

Directions

1. Group students into teams of four.

2. Give each team a "Career Guess Who" card.

3. Read aloud one of the career descriptions on the next page.

4. Group one will have an opportunity to guess first. If they are correct, place a sticker on their "Career Guess Who" card. If they are incorrect, the chance goes on to group two and so on until one of the teams guesses correctly and wins the sticker.

5. Each time a career is guessed correctly, expand and discuss additional information regarding that career and address pros and cons in the workplace.

6. Read aloud another career description and start with group two.

7. Repeat until each group has had a turn to guess first, and/or until you run out of career descriptions.

8. The team earning the most stickers wins.

Note to facilitator: The descriptions include challenging words that can be used with older students. This activity can easily be used with younger students, but consider altering the language for children under the age of ten. This list may also be enhanced.

Materials

- One "Career Guess Who" card per group (see below for pattern)
- Career Clues
- Stickers

Career Clues for "Career Guess Who"

Carpenter

I enjoy using tools to saw, shape, and fasten wood to buildings. People praise me for my creativity. I am able to work both outside and inside depending on the job at hand. I learned my trade from working as an apprentice.

Journalist

I loved Language Arts and English classes in high school and college. Social studies and current events were other favorite classes that inspired me to pursue my work. I wake up each morning to review my work, as critics often do the same. There are times that I put myself in harms way just to get a juicy story.

Chemist

I love understanding what happens when you mix things together. My favorite thing to do in elementary school was to conduct experiments. In college, my favorite subjects were math and science related. I love to learn and went to school for six more years after college and am now working in a lab and writing reports about my research.

Judge

The rights of individuals are very important to me. I seek to make sure that fairness and order exist in my place of work. I spend most of the day reading and interpreting judicial language. I spent a lot of time writing while getting my doctorate and have worked to defend and prosecute fellow citizens.

Chef

Creating and improvising are my specialty. I attended a culinary institute after high school and learned how to design, measure, and present my product as best as possible. I often distribute my product to large establishments for consumption.

Pharmacist

Science and Math are my favorite subjects. I help people feel better when they are sick. I learned a lot about the interactions of substances while in college for six years. Lately, I spend a good bit of time researching the latest products so that I understand the exact governmental laws. After passing my big exam, I was able to become licensed and work in hospitals, nursing homes, convenience stores, and drug companies.

Dentist

I like to keep things white and clean. I wear a mask to keep me from coming in contact with germs. I spent many years after college going to graduate school for my profession. I look at x-rays and give out goodies to all of my clients at the end of our meetings.

Welder

In my position, I work in very hot conditions performing sometimes dangerous operations to ensure the safety of my equipment. I cut and bind steel together and sometimes work in an assembly line fashion. Some of my favorite subjects in high school were Mechanical Drawing, Shop Class, Physics, and Math.

Electrician

I work with circuits and install, connect, and test systems. I worked as an apprentice for five years before I worked for myself. There are some safety concerns with my job, and being on my feet all day can get strenuous. When I go to people's houses and do a good job, their smiles often "Light" up the room.

Air Traffic Controller

I am responsible for the safety of many things. Each day, I must spend the day at the control center and determine weather patterns. I use radars to find the best routes for my clients. After high school, I spent a couple of years going to a specialized school before beginning my career. After completion of this school and prior to gaining my credentials from the FAA, I had to pass medical and security examinations before my 31st birthday. I spend many evenings away from my family.

Firefighter

I am often known as a first responder. I began my career as a volunteer but enjoyed my squad so much that I made it my full-time career. I know a lot about building structure and studied for many hours to pass the written test associated with my career. I continue to train for my upcoming tests of strength, physical stamina, and agility and was asked to attend the academy for additional formalized training due to my recent success on the written exam.

Engineer

In college, I took many Math and Science courses. When picking my major, I chose between Mechanical, Civil, Aerospace, Chemical, and Industrial concentrations. I work inside of an office many days but also travel to different places to observe and inspect my products. I often work long hours, sometimes spanning into the evening if a project needs completion.

What's in Your Mind?

Materials
- Small pictures of several careers
- Scissors
- Masking tape

Objective

Students will have an opportunity to discuss characteristics of different careers and use their prior knowledge to learn new information.

Directions

1. Using rolled masking tape, stick a picture of a career on each student's forehead without the student seeing the picture.

2. Participants will sit in a circle and each of them will take turns asking a yes or no question to the group about the career that is on his/her forehead. Group members will only be able to answer yes or no to each question.

3. The questions continue until one of the members successfully guesses the career on his/her forehead.

4. The leader will then facilitate a discussion around the traits that helped the participant to guess the career correctly.

✂ cut along dotted lines

Answers: Firefighter, Carpenter, Chemist/Scientist, Welder, Chef, Dentist/Dental Assistant), Electrician, Journalist/Reporter, Judge, Pharmacist, Air Traffic Controller, Architect /Engineer

Career Cluster Match Up!!!

Objective

1. Students will be able to identify which jobs fall into various career clusters.

2. Participants will begin to identify similarities between jobs in certain clusters.

Materials
- 16 empty shoe box bottoms
- Balloon label pattern
- Markers
- Scissors
- Glue
- Various shoe type cutouts – one of each per student
- Occupation/career list (see page 17)

Directions

1. Cut out a label for each box (See pages 15-16).

2. Glue the labels to the sides of the shoe boxes.

3. Explain that Career Clusters contain jobs in the same field of work that require similar skills. By understanding what types of different jobs fall into the same career cluster, you can focus your education, job training, and volunteer plans to fit the types you might like.

4. Pass out shoe cutouts to students so that each student has one of each style (See pages 15-16).

5. Have kids choose a career for each shoe cutout and label that cutout with that career.

6. On the opposite side of the cutout, have students write down 5 facts about that career.
- Job description
- Location
- Education/training needed
- Salary
- Pros/Cons

7. Sitting in a circle with the shoe boxes in the middle, have each student choose one of his/her career shoes and tell about the facts of that career. Then have that student place the shoe in the right career cluster shoe box.

8. Repeat with all of the shoes if time permits. If not, just have each student take turns putting their shoes in the designated boxes without reporting the facts.

9. Once all the shoes have been sorted into the proper shoe boxes, review the different jobs and discuss with students what types of things the jobs have in common in each particular cluster.

✂ cut along dotted lines

Agriculture, Food and Natural Resources

Jobs in this career cluster involve the production, processing, marketing, and distribution of agricultural goods. This includes food, plants, animals, fabrics, wood, and crops. Workers in this career cluster might work on a farm, ranch, orchard, greenhouse, or plant nursery. Or, they might work in a clinic or laboratory as a scientist or engineer.

Architecture and Construction

Jobs in this career cluster involve designing, planning, managing, constructing and maintaining buildings and other structures. This includes working on highways, bridges, houses, and buildings. Workers in this career cluster might create the designs or plans for new structures. Or, they might use the plans to build it or manage the workers on the project.

Arts, Audio/Video Technology and Communications

Jobs in this career cluster involve using creativity in designing, producing, exhibiting, performing, writing, and publishing. Workers in this career cluster might work for an audience as a performer or artist, such as a painter, dancer, sculptor, actor, or singer. Or, they might work behind the scenes to make a performance successful, in a role such as a set designer, editor, broadcast technician, or camera operator.

Business, Management, and Administration

Jobs in this career cluster give the support needed to make a business run. These jobs involve planning, organizing, directing and evaluating business functions. Workers in this career cluster might check employee time records or train new employees. Or, they might work as a top executive and provide the overall direction for a company or department.

Education and Training

Jobs in this career cluster involve guiding and training people. Jobs in this career cluster generally influence young lives, such as a teacher or school counselor. Or, they can support the work of a classroom, coach sports activities, or lead community classes.

Finance

Jobs in this career cluster involve working with money. Workers in this career cluster might be responsible for financial and investment planning, banking, insurance, and business financial management.

Government and Public Administration

Jobs in this career cluster involve executing governmental functions. Workers in this career cluster could work in national, state, or local government. Government and Public Administration workers might inspect new or remodeled buildings for safety, help people file the paperwork for a marriage license, or create proposals for urban development.

Heath Science

Jobs in this career cluster promote health and wellness. Health Science workers might diagnose and treat injuries and diseases, dispense medication, or work in a laboratory to find cures for illnesses.

Hospitality and Tourism

Jobs in this career cluster involve the operation of restaurants and other foodservices, lodging, attractions, recreation events and travel related services. Workers in this career cluster might work at a restaurant, resort, sports arena, theme park, museum, or hotel.

Human Services

Jobs in this career cluster involve helping individuals and families to meet their personal needs. Human Services workers might work in a government office, hospital, nonprofit agency, nursing home, spa, hotel, or school. Or, they might work in their own home.

Information Technology

Jobs in this career cluster involve working with computers. Workers in this career cluster might work with computer hardware, software, multimedia, or network systems. They might design new computer equipment or work on new computer games.

Law, Public Safety, Corrections and Security

Jobs in this career cluster involve providing legal, public safety, protective services and homeland security. Workers in this career cluster might guard the public and enforce the law as a police officer or security guard. Or, they might provide fire protection as a firefighter. Other workers can provide legal services to people who commit crimes.

Manufacturing

Jobs in this career cluster involve working with products and equipment. Workers in this career cluster might design a new product, decide how the product will be made, or make the product. They might work with heavy equipment and machinery to make goods such as cars, computers, appliances, airplanes, electronic devices or even clothing and jewelry.

Marketing, Sales, and Services

Jobs in this career cluster help businesses to sell products. Workers in this career cluster might advertise and promote products so customers want to buy them, or they might work in a store to sell products and services to customers.

Science, Technology, Engineering, and Mathematics

Jobs in this career cluster involve doing scientific research in laboratories or in the field. Workers in this career cluster might plan or design products or systems, or try to solve complex mathematical problems.

Transportation, Distribution, Logistics

Jobs in this career cluster involve planning, management, and movement of people, materials, and goods by road, pipeline, air, rail and water. Workers in this career cluster might work as a driver, pilot, engineer, or captain. They might repair or maintain the vehicles, trains, planes, and ships that move people and products, or they might work behind the scenes to make sure the products and people get to the right place on time.

Occupation/Career List

Agriculture, Food and Natural Resources

- Animal Breeders
- Farm and Ranch Managers
- Agricultural and Food Science Technicians
- Foresters
- Soil and Water Conservationists
- Fishers and Related Fishing Workers
- Nursery and Greenhouse Managers
- Hunters and Trappers

Architecture and Construction

- Architects
- Carpenters
- Cement Masons and Concrete Finishers
- Construction and Building Inspectors
- Electricians
- Plumbers
- Interior Designers
- Pipelayers

Arts, Audio/Video Technology and Communications

- Actors
- Audio and Video Equipment Technicians
- Writers and Authors
- Choreographers
- Fine Artists, Including Painters, Sculptors, and Illustrators
- Musicians and Singers
- Animators and Graphic Designers
- Directors - Stage, Motion Pictures, Television, and Radio

Business, Management, and Administration

- Business Managers
- Chief Executives
- Human Resources Specialists
- Executive Secretaries and Administrative Assistants
- General and Operations Managers
- Market Research Analysts and Marketing Specialists
- Office Clerks
- Payroll and Timekeeping Clerks

Education and Training

- Teachers
- School Principals
- School Counselors
- Tutors
- Librarians
- Coaches and Scouts
- Special Education Teachers
- College or University Professor

Finance

- Accountants
- Financial Analysts
- Insurance Underwriters
- Loan Counselors
- Bill and Account Collectors
- Insurance Appraisers
- Tax Preparers
- Personal Financial Advisors

Government and Public Administration

- City and Regional Planning Aides
- Court Clerks
- Urban and Regional Planners
- Special Forces Officers
- Government Property Inspectors and Investigators
- Infantry Officers
- Licensing Examiners and Inspectors
- Surveying and Mapping Technicians

Heath Science

- Ambulance Drivers and Attendants
- Doctors
- Chiropractors
- Critical Care Nurses
- Dentists
- Hearing Aid Specialists
- Pharmacists
- Veterinarians

Hospitality and Tourism

- Amusement and Recreation Attendants
- Chefs and Head Cooks
- Food Service Managers
- Gaming Managers
- Interpreters and Translators
- Tour Guides and Escorts
- Travel Agents
- Ushers, Lobby Attendants, and Ticket Takers

Human Services

- Mental Health Counselors
- Clergy
- Childcare Workers and Nannies
- Fitness Trainers and Aerobics Instructors
- Personal Care Aides
- Rehabilitation Counselors
- Customer Service Representatives
- Massage Therapists

Information Technology

- Computer and Information Researchers
- Computer Programmers
- Computer User Support Specialists
- Software Developers, Applications and Systems Software
- Video Game Designers
- Web Developers
- Information Technology Security Analysts
- Computer Database Administrators

Law, Public Safety, Corrections and Security

- Court Reporters
- Detectives and Criminal Investigators
- Fire Inspectors and Investigators
- Judges
- Paralegals and Legal Assistants
- Security Guards
- Transportation Security Screeners
- Lawyers

Manufacturing

- Aircraft Structure, Surfaces, Rigging, and Systems Assemblers
- Engine and Other Machine Assemblers
- Welders, Cutters, Solderers, and Brazers
- Fabric and Apparel Patternmakers
- Glass Blowers, Molders, Benders, and Finishers
- Robotics Technicians
- Sewing Machine Operators
- Jewelers and Precious Stone and Metal Workers

Marketing, Sales, and Services

- Advertising and Promotions Managers
- Door-To-Door Sales Workers, News and Street Vendors, and Related Workers
- Cashiers
- Marketing Managers
- Real Estate Brokers
- Retail Salespersons
- Telemarketers
- Models

Science, Technology, Engineering, and Mathematics

- Aerospace Engineers
- Chemists
- Geographers
- Physicists
- Statisticians
- Zoologists and Wildlife Biologists
- Electrical Engineers
- Mathematicians

Transportation, Distribution, Logistics

- Air Traffic Controllers
- Airline Pilots, Copilots, and Flight Engineers
- Aviation Inspectors
- Commercial Drivers
- Flight Attendants
- Tractor-Trailer Truck Drivers
- Railroad Conductors
- Ship and Boat Captains

Career Matching Game

Objective

Students will learn about different jobs, the type of schooling needed for those jobs, and the amount of money they might earn in different careers.

Directions

1. Give each student a copy of the Career Matching Game Worksheet (page 19). Use your pencil to draw a line from the Job Title to the Type of Preparation for that job and then to the Average Salary of the job. Use a different colored pencil for each job title.

2. Please note that more than one job title will fall under each type of education/training and salary.

3. After completing the worksheet, use the answer key (page 20) to review your answers.

Materials

- Colored Pencils
- Career Matching Game Worksheet (1 per student)
- Career Matching Game Answer Key (for teacher to review completed worksheets)

Just for fun! Choose one job title of your choice and look up the specific prevailing wage for that particular job in your geographical location on the O*Net website **http://www.onetonline.org**.

TITLE	DESCRIPTION	SCHOOLING / PREPARATION	AVERAGE ANNUAL SALARY	SALARY RANGE
Accountant	Analyze financial information and prepare financial reports.	Bachelor's Degree	$65,080	$60,000 - $70,000
Aerospace Engineer	Design, construct, and test aircraft, missile, and spacecraft components.	Bachelor's Degree	$103,870	$100,000 +
Animal Scientist	Research the genetics, nutrition, reproduction, and growth of domestic farm animals.	Doctorate Degree	$64,260	$60,000 - $70,000
Auto mechanic	Repair systems or components on vehicles.	Vocational or Trade School	$36,710	$30,000 – $40,000
Carpenter	Construct and repair structures and fixtures of wood using hand tools and power tools.	High School Diploma or less	$40,000	$30,000 – $40,000
Chiropractor	Assess, treat, and care for patients by moving bones in the spine.	Doctorate Degree	$65,300	$60,000 - $70,000
Economist	Conduct research to address economic problems.	Master's Degree	$93,070	$90,000 - $100,000
Electrician	Install, maintain, and repair electrical wiring, equipment, and fixtures.	Vocational or Trade School	$50,510	$50,000 - $60,000
Farmer or Rancher	Plan, direct, or coordinate the management or operation of farms, ranches, or greenhouses.	High School Diploma or less	$70,110	$70,000 - $80,000
Fashion Designer	Design clothing and accessories.	Associate's Degree	$63,760	$60,000 - $70,000
Graphic Designer	Design or create graphics for commercial or promotional needs.	Bachelor's Degree	$44,830	$40,000 – $50,000
Model	Model garments or other apparel and accessories for prospective buyers.	High School Diploma or less	$19,040	$20,000 or less
Pilot	Fly and navigate aircrafts.	Bachelor's Degree	$115,190	$100,000 +
Plumber	Assemble, install, or repair pipes, fittings, or fixtures of heating, water, or drainage systems,	Vocational or Trade School	$50,108	$50,000 - $60,000
Postal Mail Carrier	Sort mail for delivery. Deliver mail on established route by vehicle or on foot.	High School Diploma	$56,490	$50,000 - $60,000
Private investigators and Detectives	Gather, analyze, compile and report information regarding individuals or detect occurrences of unlawful acts.	Vocational schools or an Associate's Degree.	$46,250	$40,000 – $50,000
School Counselor	Counsel individuals or groups and provide educational, social-emotional, and career guidance.	Master's degree	$53,600	$50,000 - $60,000
Surgeon	Physicians who treat diseases, injuries, and deformities by surgical methods.	Medical Degree	$187,200	$100,000 +
Teacher	Teach students in one or more subjects in public or private schools.	Bachelor's Degree	$53,940	$50,000 - $60,000
Video Game Designers	Design core features of video games.	Bachelor's Degree	$82,340	$80,000 - $90,000
Waiters and Waitresses	Take orders and serve food and beverages to patrons at tables in dining establishment.	High School Diploma or less	$18,590	$20,000 or less

Career Matching Game Worksheet

Using different colored pencils, draw a line matching the career with the type of preparation and salary range.

JOB TITLE	TYPE OF PREPARATION	AVERAGE SALARY OF THIS JOB
Accountant		
Aerospace Engineer		
Animal Scientist		
Auto mechanic	High School Diploma or less	$30,000 or less
Carpenter		
Chiropractor		
Economist	Associates Degree, Trade School, or Vocational School	$30,000 – $40,000
Electrician		
Farmer or Rancher		$40,000 – $50,000
Fashion Designer		
Graphic Designer	Bachelor's Degree	$50,000 - $60,000
Model		
Pilot		$60,000 - $70,000
Plumber		
Postal Mail Carrier	Master's Degree	$70,000 - $80,000
Private Investigators and Detectives		$80,000 - $90,000
School Counselor		
Surgeon	Medical Degree or Doctorate Degree	$90,000 - $100,000
Teacher		
Video Game Designer		$100,000 +
Waiters and Waitresses		

20

Career Charades (for small groups)

✂ cut along dotted lines

HOUSE PAINTER

CROSSING GUARD

DOCTOR

CONDUCTOR

TEACHER

Materials

- Charade Suggestion Cards
- Hat/bag/box or other container to hold the cards
- 1 minute timer

Objective

Students will demonstrate their understanding of the tasks involved in various jobs by acting out those tasks while others try to guess the job.

Directions

1. Photocopy the Career Charades Cards (this page and next) and cut out each card. Place the cards in a box/bag/hat or other container that the students can pick from.

2. Explain to the group that they will be playing a guessing game. One person will act out a certain career (the "actor") and the rest of the group (the "guessers") will try to guess what he/she is doing.

3. Invite one actor to the front of the room and ask her or him to pick a career out of the hat but do not show the rest of the group.

4. Start the timer for one minute and invite the actor to get started.

5. Each actor will have one minute to act out what he or she sees on the card while the guessers try to figure out what career they are acting out. Guessers may call out their guesses as the actor is acting.

6. The actor may NOT use any words! He/she can only use gestures and make sounds. If the actor is having trouble thinking of what to act out, they can look at the picture on their card for clues.

NOTE: You may wish to split the guessers into two teams and have them compete for the most correct guesses.

CHEF

SINGER/ RAPPER

ARTIST

DETECTIVE

PROFESSIONAL ATHLETE

MAIL CARRIER

RESEARCHER/ SCIENTIST

FILMMAKER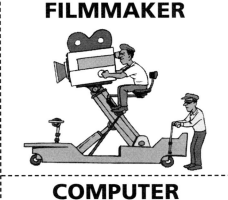

SHIP CAPTAIN

PROFESSIONAL DANCER

COMPUTER PROGRAMMER

DENTIST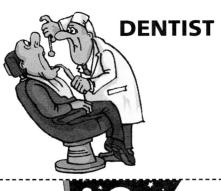

LIBRARIAN

PHOTOGRAPHER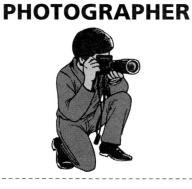

ASTRONOMER

My Career Recipe Builder

Objective

1. Students will begin to examine some of the job traits that closely match their personalities and preferences.

2. Students will gain awareness of some potential careers that fit their unique characteristics.

Directions

1. Students answer questions to fill out their career "ingredients."

2. Once they determine the individual ingredients, have students mix the ingredients together to create a recipe for a possible great career fit.

Materials

• Pencils
• Career Recipe Worksheet (one for each student
• Recipe outcomes (for facilitators)

Career Recipe Worksheet

Use this worksheet to determine the various ingredients for your career recipe. Write which answer best fits you (bold in caps) to each question in the correspondingly numbered **Ingredient** space to the right.

1. Do you like to spend your time **INSIDE** or **OUTSIDE**?

2. Do you prefer to work in a **GROUP** or **INDEPENDENTLY**?

3. Do you like to be the **LEADER** or do you like to **FOLLOW DIRECTIONS** from other people?

4. Do you prefer to do **PHYSICAL** work or **NON-PHYSICAL** work?

Ingredient 1:
_____

Ingredient 2:
_____

Ingredient 3:
_____

Ingredient 4:
_____

Mixing all of your ingredients together, here are some possible jobs that might interest you.

Inside or Outside	Group or Independently	Physical or Non-Physical	Leader or Follow Others	
Inside	Group	Physical	Leader	Aerobics Instructor, Warehouse Manager, Choreographer, Physical Therapist
Inside	Group	Physical	Follow Others	Assembly Line Worker, Hockey Player
Inside	Group	Non-Physical	Leader	Marketing Team Leader, Air Traffic Controller, Accountant, Teacher, Librarian
Inside	Group	Non-Physical	Follow Others	Staff Reporter, Editor, Court Reporter
Inside	Independently	Physical	Leader	Carpet Installer, Painter
Inside	Independently	Physical	Follow Others	Nurse, Archivists
Inside	Independently	Non-Physical	Leader	Broadcast News Analyst, Copy Writers, Lawyer, Therapist
Inside	Independently	Non-Physical	Follow Others	Research Scientist
Outside	Group	Physical	Leader	Hiking Tour Guide, Umpires, Referees, and Other Sports Officials, Highway Maintenance Worker Manager, Emergency Medical Technicians and Paramedics, Environmentalist
Outside	Group	Physical	Follow Others	Logging Equipment Operators, Miner, Cement Mason, Pipe Fitters and Steamfitters, Refuse and Recyclable Material Collectors, Archeologist
Outside	Group	Non-Physical	Leader	Painting Instructor, Public Relations Specialists
Outside	Group	Non-Physical	Follow Others	Surveyor, Project Manager/Engineer,
Outside	Independently	Physical	Leader	Electrician, Crossing Guards, Meter Readers, Golf Pro, Tour Guide
Outside	Independently	Physical	Follow Others	Door-To-Door Sales Worker
Outside	Independently	Non-Physical	Leader	Floral Designers, Reporters and Correspondents
Outside	Independently	Non-Physical	Follow Others	Truck Driver, Subway Operator, Air Traffic Controller, Car Salesman, Drivers Ed Instructor

No Thanks!

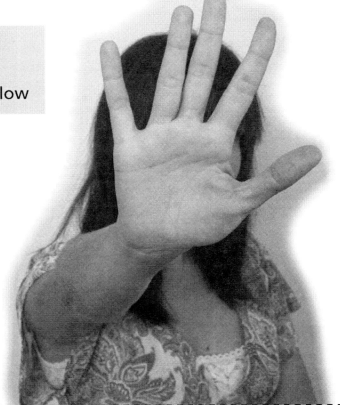

Materials
- Pencil
- Activity sheet below

Objective

1. Help students differentiate their strengths and interests with different careers.

2. Help students rule out certain careers.

Directions

1. Identify at least one specific career in which they have no interest.

2. Fill out the following information about this career:

"No, Thanks!"

A career that I am **NOT** interested in is:

_____

Here are three things about this career that I know:

    1. _____

    2. _____

    3. _____

Here are three things I know about me that would **NOT** make this a good fit:

    1. _____

    2. _____

    3. _____

---

3. Present this information to others to request additional information that may be of interest.

My Résumé

NAME_____   DATE _____

A. Career Objective

- What do you want to do when you work? (Consider these for example: save lives, participate in sports or build things?)

When I work, I want to:

_____
_____
_____

B. Education

Current grade in school: _____

Special Achievements in School:_____

_____
_____
_____

Education Plan (What you need to do for what you want to be.)

What level of education would you like to have? (check all that apply)

- ☐ Finish high school
- ☐ Finish college
- ☐ Finish trade school
- ☐ Join the military

C. Skills

Skills allow you to do things well. Some examples of skills include: drawing, music, athletics, telling stories or jokes, working well with others, leadership, helping others, being a team player, good with technology, great memory, good with numbers, etc.

List the skills you have: _____

_____
_____
_____

D. Experience

As a kid, your working experience is probably limited to making your bed, taking out the garbage, mowing the lawn, and other chores. You have to start somewhere and make a point to take steps every year to develop your experiences. Experience is a good thing! Even though making your bed seems like a real pain, it is a good start for kids to assume responsibility and become more independent. Becoming independent is an important life skill that will help others to trust you. This will not only make your parents very proud and happy, but it will make you feel more confident in yourself; you'll then be better prepared for future challenges in life.

continued on next page

Things I do to help at home:

_____
_____
_____
_____
_____
_____
_____

Things I do to help at school:

_____
_____
_____
_____
_____
_____
_____
_____
_____

E. Personal Interests:

The Personal section is probably the easiest part of developing your résumé, because it is about the things you like to do outside of school and work. This section helps people get to know you as a person, beyond your education and experience. This is an area that is important for you to start working on now. It can start with sports, music, arts or community clubs and evolve over the years as your interests change.

Sports I like: _____
_____
_____
_____

Clubs/Teams I belong to: _____
_____
_____
_____

Things I Like to Read: _____
_____
_____
_____

Other fun things I like to do:_____
_____
_____
_____

Job Application

APPLICANT INFORMATION

Last Name	First	M.I.	Date

Street Address		City	Zip Code

Email Address	Date Available	Social Security No.

Position Applied for

Are you a citizen of the United States? YES NO	If no, are you authorized to work in the U.S.? YES NO
Have you ever worked for this company? YES NO	If so, when?
Have you ever been convicted of a felony? YES NO	If yes, explain:

EDUCATION

Elementary			
From	To	Did you pass? YES NO	
College		Address	
From	To	Did you graduate? YES NO	Degree

REFERENCES

Full Name	Relationship

Why this person?

PREVIOUS EMPLOYMENT

Company	Phone ( )
Address	Supervisor

Job Title	Starting Salary $	Ending Salary $

Responsibilities

From	To	Reason for Leaving

May we contact your previous supervisor for a reference? YES NO

DISCLAIMER AND SIGNATURE

I certify that my answers are true and complete to the best of my knowledge.

If this application leads to employment, I understand that false or misleading information in my application or interview may result in my release.

Signature _____   Date _____

Mock Interview

Objective

- Students will prepare and practice interviewing for a job by completing a mock interview.
- Students will provide a complete portfolio (including a résumé and job application) to the interviewer.
- Students will write a thank you note to the interviewer.
- Students will receive a mock letter indicating if they would/would not be hired for the job, complete with suggestions for improvement.

Directions

1. Provide teachers with information about a job and ask the teachers to interview students for the position. They can use the following interview questions:
   - What is the job you are applying for?
   - Why would you like this job?
   - Why are you the best applicant for this job?
   - How is your attendance at school?
   - Are you dependable? Do you complete and turn in schoolwork on time?
   - What are your other interests/activities?
   - In what areas would you like to grow?
   - What do you do to overcome challenges?
   - Are you a team player?

2. Have students research their jobs of choice, and complete a résumé and job application for their selected job to bring to the interview. (See Tips for Interviewing sheet, next page)

3. Encourage students to dress up for their interview. (First impressions count!)

4. Send students a reminder about their mock interview. (Use the form on the next page or create your own.)

5. After they interview, have students write and deliver a thank you note to the teacher who interviewed them.

6. Have teachers send a letter to the students indicating whether or not they got the job. Encourage the teachers to give the students feedback on how they did during the interview and how they can improve in the future.

Tips for Interviewing

Before the Interview

- Complete/update your résumé.
- Use your best penmanship! **Neatness counts!**
- Research the job in advance.
- Think about how you will fit into the job. List the skills you have to offer the position.
- Be prepared to ask any questions you may have.
- Dress appropriately. **Neatness and cleanliness are very important.**
- Be sure you are on time for the interview.

At the Interview

- Have confidence in yourself. Present yourself well. **SMILE!**
- Shake hands firmly. Say "Hi. How are you? I am _____..."
- Be pleasant, and try to relax. Avoid nervous habits.
- Maintain good posture.
- Think before you speak.
- Look at the interviewer when talking.
- Answer questions completely; do not just give "yes" or "no" answers.
- Show enthusiasm and interest in the job.
- Sell yourself! Turn weaknesses into strengths!
- Shake hands when leaving. Say, "Thank you for your time and consideration. I have enjoyed meeting you."

Potential Questions You May Be Asked

- What is the job you are applying for?
- Why would you like this job?
- Why are you the best applicant for this job?
- How is your attendance at school?
- Are you dependable? Do you complete and turn in schoolwork on time?
- What are your other interests/activities?

✂ cut along dotted lines

Interview reminder sheet:

To: _____ (student)

From: _____ (teacher)

Your job interview is scheduled for _____ (time) at _____ (place). Remember, when you go to a job interview, you should look nice and professional. I am not telling you to wear a dress or a suit, but please dress nicely that day, as you will be practicing what it is like to be on a real job interview.

A few tips in preparing for the interview:

1. Think about WHY you want this job.
2. Think about what makes YOU the best person for this job.
3. What is one fact you know about the job?
4. Stating your name, making eye contact, and a firm hand shake are important.

Annual Career Fair Idea

Dear Parent(s)/Guardian(s),

As you know, career education is very important. This year, your children have participated in a variety of activities that are centered around their future careers. For example, they have completed a résumé and job application to not only learn the components of each but also to experience the process of personal reflection and career exploration. They have also participated in a mock interview for a job of their choice where they "dressed up," provided a complete portfolio to the interviewer, and received a letter indicating if they would have been hired for the job. These valuable lessons have encouraged awareness of potential careers, highlighted the importance of lifelong learning, and set precedence for being a hard-working student.

This year, I would like to have a Career Fair for the students. The concept would involve parents by highlighting the parents' careers. If you agree to participate, then you would be asked to:

• Dress in clothing you normally wear on the job

• Create an informal, 2-3 minute presentation about your job

• Discuss WHY you chose that career

• State what, if any, continuing education was needed to perform the job

• Explain to students the importance of hard work and dedication to school

• Bring any tools you use on the job

This Career Fair cannot be a success without your help. Please consider attending our annual Career Fair at _____ (location) on _____ (date) from _____ (time). Once I have received your R.S.V.P. (the section below), I will create a small poster that includes your name and career. The students will have a list of the careers and prepared questions about that career. Thank you for considering this opportunity as good community outreach for our students! Please contact me at _____ if you have any questions or comments. Return by _____ (date).

Sincerely,

Teacher/School Counselor

✂ cut here and keep top portion
- -

Count Me In!

I would like to participate in the Career Fair by featuring my career. I understand my

responsibilities as listed above. I will arrive at _____ (location)

by _____ (time) to set up.

Name: _____

Career: _____

☐ I will need an electrical outlet. (Please check if applicable.)

Sample Career Fair Student Worksheet

Name _____

Teacher _____

Directions

Answer these questions while listening to each parent speak about his or her career.

1. What is one tool, or piece of equipment that the presenter uses?

_____

2. Why did the presenter choose this career?

_____

_____

_____

3. What is one activity this person does at their job?

_____

_____

_____

4. What training did the presenter need for his/her career?

_____

_____

_____

5. What level of education is needed for this job?

_____

_____

6. Did the presenter go to college?

_____

7. Does it sound like the presenter enjoys his/her job?

_____

_____

8. What is one new thing you learned about this career?

_____

_____

What career did you enjoy hearing about the most?

_____

_____

_____

What did you like about the Career Fair?

_____

_____

_____

What is something that surprised you about one of the jobs?

_____

_____

_____

What job(s) sounded the most exciting to you? Why

_____

_____

_____

What job(s) sounded the least exciting to you? Why

_____

_____

_____